POLLY AND THE W

What a treat to have a ch   ·
ingenious ways in which C   ... outwit the
Stupid Wolf!

The original collection of stories about the feisty Polly
and the charming, irrepressibly confident and ever-hungry
Wolf was the bedrock of my childhood reading. I loved
to be thrillingly scared in each story, and then deliciously
reassured that the Wolf would never quite catch Polly even
though, at times, he gets so very close to it.

Fortunately, Catherine's Storr's seam of invention runs
deep; she has plenty of equally entertaining variations on
the theme for this book, too. The premise this time is that
the Wolf, having learnt a thing or two from his earlier
bruising encounters, is now determined to turn the tables.
Disgusted at being labelled Stupid he begins by setting his
hand to a new collection of stories to right the wrong: The
Clever Wolf and Poor Stupid Polly.

Alas, poor Wolf – and Catherine Storr makes sure that
as long as Polly remains safe she and the readers do feel
sorry for him – he has no better luck this time round,
despite some sophisticated tricks and disguises. But in
this book there is a bonus; not only is the original joke
as strong as ever, but there is also an additional layer of
humour as Wolf's behaviour is now a response to his
earlier attempts to get Polly – as well as to the injustice of
traditional fiction.

How Polly stays safe in these stories was a matter of
great importance to me. Perhaps that was especially so

because the setting of the stories was very close to my home as the illustrations vividly demonstrated: I posted letters in the same letter box as Polly and I sat on the same park bench. But for all readers, Polly's reality of home and family juxtaposed with the fantasy of Wolf makes this book a delight.

Julia Eccleshare

ABOUT CATHERINE STORR

Catherine Storr was born in London and practiced as a psychiatrist before becoming a writer. She believed – and felt that children understood – that fantasy and reality were not opposites, but different ways of looking at the same thing. Catherine Storr wrote over one hundred books for children, including many retellings of myths and legends. *Polly and the Wolf Again* is the second Polly book – the sequel to *Clever Polly and the Stupid Wolf*.

ABOUT THE ILLUSTRATOR

A Londoner, Marjorie-Ann Watts trained as a painter and illustrator, worked for a time as an art editor and typographer, and has written and illustrated many books for children.

P... THE WOLF AGAIN

Catherine Storr

ILLUSTRATED BY
MARJORIE-ANN WATTS

Also by Catherine Storr in Jane Nissen Books:

CLEVER POLLY AND THE STUPID WOLF

JANE NISSEN BOOKS
Swan House
Chiswick Mall
London W4 2PS

First published in Great Britain by Faber and Faber 1957
Published by Jane Nissen Books 2011

Design
Nigel Hazle

Cover design
Chris Inns

Printed & bound in Great Britain by the MPG Books Group

A CIP catalogue record of this book is available from the
British Library

ISBN 978–1-903252-38-3

Contents

━━━━━━━━━◦◦◦◦◦◦◦━━━━━━━━━

The Clever Wolf and Poor Stupid Little Polly (I)

T he wolf sat at home in his kitchen, where he usually enjoyed himself so much; his elbows were on the table, and he was chewing, but there was no feeling of peace, of comfortable fullness, of not being likely to be hungry again for several hours, which was how the wolf liked to feel in his own house.

The table was covered with sheets of paper. Some of them had only a word or two written on them, some had a whole sentence. Most of them were blank.

Presently the wolf sighed, spat out the object he had been chewing—it was a pencil—and tried again. On a large clean sheet of paper he wrote, laboriously:

"One day the Clever Wolf caught Polly and ate her all up!"

He stopped. He read what he had written. Then he read it again. He put the pencil back between his teeth and began to search among the sheets of paper for something. When he found it, he opened it flat on the table and leant over it, spelling out the longer words as he read. It was a book.

The Clever Wolf and Poor Stupid Little Polly (I)

But reading did not seem much more satisfactory than writing. Every now and then the wolf snarled, and at last he shut the book up with a snap and pushed it away from him; but as he did so, his eyes fell on the cover, and the name of the book, printed there in large black letters:

CLEVER POLLY AND THE STUPID WOLF

"It's so unfair!" he muttered angrily to himself, "*Clever Polly*, indeed! Just because she's managed to escape me for a time. And calling me stupid! Me! Why, I always used to win when we played Hide the Piglet as wolf cubs. 'Stupid Wolf!' I'll show them. I'll write a book full of stories which will show how clever I am—far cleverer than that silly little Polly. I'll start the story of my life now, and then everyone will be able to see that it's not me that is stupid."

The Clever Wolf and Poor Stupid Little Polly (I)

He pulled another sheet of paper towards him.

"I was born", he began writing in his untidy sprawling hand, "in a large and comfortable hole, in the year——"

He stopped.

"Well, I know I'm about eleven," he said to himself. "So if I take eleven away from now, I shall know when I was born. Eleven away from . . . eleven away from. . . . What am I taking eleven away from?"

"I'll do it with beans!" he thought, encouraging himself. "It's always easier with beans."

Leaving his pencil on the table, he got up and fetched a large canister of dried beans from a shelf over the stove. He shook a small shower out on the table: one or two fell on the floor.

"Nine, ten, eleven," counted the wolf. He tipped the spare beans back into the canister.

"But I'm taking eleven away from something," he remembered. He looked doubtfully into the tin and tipped it a little to see how full it was. The beans made an agreeable rattling sound as they slid about inside, and the wolf shook the canister gently several times to hear it again.

"There seem to be an awful lot of beans in there," he said aloud. "I wonder just what I've got to take eleven away from?"

He sat down to consider the point. Could it be eleven? He spread the eleven beans out on the table and looked at them. Then he took eleven beans off the table, counting them one by one.

"Eleven away leaves none. So eleven years ago was nothing. The year nothing. It seems a very long time ago."

The wolf was puzzled. It did certainly seem a very long time ago, but it still didn't sound quite right. He could not remember ever having seen a book which gave as a date the year nothing.

"It can't be right," he decided. "It must be eleven away from something else. I wonder what it is? Who could I ask to tell me?"

There was, of course, only one answer to this, and five minutes later the wolf had walked down the path through the garden to Polly's front door and was ringing her bell.

"I'll talk to you from up here if you don't mind," said Polly's voice from the first floor window. "Yes, Wolf, what can I do for you today?"

"You can tell me what I have to take eleven away from."

"Eleven? Why eleven?"

"Because that is how old I am."

"Why do you want to take how old you are away from anything?"

"Because I want to know what year it was."

"What year what was?"

"The year I was born in, of course. Silly!" said the wolf triumphantly. "I said it was Silly Polly and you are! What do I take it away from?"

"Nineteen seventy-five."

"And what do I have to do with it?" the wolf asked, now thoroughly muddled.

"You take that away from it."

"What's That?"

"Eleven. Well, that's what you said," Polly answered, a little confused herself.

"Don't go away," pleaded the wolf. "Let me get it straight in my head. I take eleven away from nineteen and then from seventy-five and then———"

"No, stupid. Not from nineteen, from nineteen hundred and seventy-five; and then the answer is the year you were born in!"

"Nineteen hundred!" said the wolf, appalled.

"And seventy-five."

"Nineteen hundred and seventy-five. I don't think I've got enough beans," said the wolf gloomily.

"I don't see how beans come into it," Polly said. "It's years, you're counting in, not beans."

"It's beans while I'm actually counting," the wolf said firmly. "And you're sure the answer is the year I was born?"

"Certain."

"Thank you. Good morning," the wolf called over his shoulder, as he trotted away down the garden path. He went home, sat down at his kitchen table and began to count out beans.

"A hundred and thirty-three, a hundred and thirty-four, a hundred and thirty-five .... Bother."

The hundred and thirty-sixth bean was a very highly polished one. It slipped out of the wolf's paw, leapt nimbly into the air, fell on the floor, and rolled under the cooking stove.

"Bother, bother, BOTHER!" the wolf said out loud. He looked into the canister. There were only seven or eight beans left: he could not afford to lose one. He got down from his chair and lay flat on his front on the floor to look for the missing bean. It lay out of reach, right at the back of the cooker, against the wall, in company with a burnt chestnut and a very dirty toasting fork.

"My toasting fork!" the wolf exclaimed, delighted to see it again: it had been missing for several months. He retrieved the fork, dusted it with his tail, and used it to poke out the bean.

The wolf dusted the bean, said solemnly out loud, "One hundred and thirty-six," and put it on the table.

He gave a triumphant wave of his useful tail. Several beans were swept off the table and disappeared under various pieces of furniture.

"Oh—!" cried the wolf enraged. He sat down at the table, staring angrily at the remaining beans. He tipped up the canister and added the rest of the beans to the pile he had already counted.

"A hundred and thirty-seven, a hundred and thirty-eight, a hundred and.... What's the use when I want nineteen hundred and something? I'll never be able to count the whole lot!"

He absent-mindedly put the last bean in his mouth. It wasn't too bad. He ate another.

"Easier with a spoon," he murmured, a minute or two later, and going to the dresser fetched a battered table spoon. With its help he ate another two dozen beans fairly quickly.

"That's funny!" he thought after the second spoonful. "I believe I generally eat these cooked. Very absent-minded I seem to be getting."

He fetched a saucepan, filled it with water, and put it on the fire. When the water was boiling he tossed in the remaining beans, salt, pepper and herbs. He fried some rashers of bacon, an onion and a few mushrooms in a pan, and when everything was cooked he mixed them into a glorious mess together, added a tomato and, in a very few mouthfuls, swallowed the lot.

"Ah," he said, wiping his mouth on the back of his paw, "that's better. Now, let me see—What was I doing?"

He looked round the kitchen and his eye fell on the empty canister.

"Oh!" he said aloud.

"Bother!"

"Never mind," he said. "They tasted much better than they counted. Besides it would have taken me ages to get up to nineteen hundred and seventy-five. I'd never have had time to write anything. After all what does it matter what year it was, I was born? I'm here now, that's the important thing."

He picked up the last sheet of paper he had written on and tore it across several times. Then, sitting down, he pulled another towards him and wrote in a bolder hand:

THE CLEVER WOLF AND POOR STUPID POLLY

"Fortunately" (the wolf wrote), "I was born."

The Clever Wolf and Poor Stupid Little Polly (II)

A few days later Polly was looking longingly in at the window of her nearest bookshop, rehearsing to herself what she would buy if she had enough money, when she realized that someone large and dark was standing by her side. The wolf was gazing through the glass and was murmuring the titles aloud to himself.

"*Fairy Tales*. Hmm. *Well-Known Fairy Tales*. If they're well known already, who wants another book about them? *Grimm Fairy Tales*—that sounds more interesting. I like grim stories as long as they're really frightening and full of crunching bones and blood and things!"

"Don't be beastly, Wolf," Polly said, rather sharply.

The wolf jumped.

"You frightened me," he said, reproachfully. "I didn't know you were there."

"I was here first," Polly reminded him.

"I daresay. I was looking at the books and I stopped

noticing you. When I get my nose into a good book," the wolf went on dreamily, "I get carried away."

"Don't show off, Wolf," Polly said. "I know you can read, but I don't believe you ever get lost in a book unless it's a cookery book. When I was in your house there wasn't a book to be seen."

"I get them all out of the library," the wolf said, hastily. "And anyhow now I'm not just reading, I'm writing a book."

"Oh, Wolf!" cried Polly, very much impressed. "How wonderful. What's it about?"

"Us," the wolf said. "Well, me really. Mostly me, but a little you. Only you don't last very long, of course."

"Why of course?"

"Because I eat you up. Very soon. Because in my book I

am Clever and you are Stupid. It's quite different from that silly book that was written about us before."

"It must be."

"This," said the wolf, puffing out his chest, "is terrific. It's a Guide to Wolves on how to catch conceited little girls who pretend to be clever."

"I'd like to read it, please," Polly said.

"Well—" the wolf said, shifting uneasily from one leg to another. "It's not as easy as it sounds. Have you ever written a book, Polly?"

"No. I've written letters."

"So have I. Dozens. Hundreds. If I added up all the letters I'd written there'd be plenty of whole words among them, too. But still, have you ever tried to write a book?"

"I wrote the beginning of a story once," Polly said.

"Pooh!" cried the wolf, "the beginning! That's the easy part. Anyone can begin a story—you just say, 'Once upon a time there was a nice juicy little girl', and there you are."

"Is it the ending you can't do?" Polly asked.

The wolf looked thoughtful. "Not exactly," he said, "I think it's the middle. I always seem to get to the end quicker than I meant to, and then the story seems too short. How long would you think a book ought to be, Polly?"

Polly thought hard. "About a hundred pages," she suggested.

"Oh NO!" the wolf said, horrified. "Not a hundred pages of writing. A short book, Polly."

"Oh, I see," Polly said. "Well—twenty pages?"

"That's an awful lot," the wolf said, sadly.

"It couldn't be less than ten," Polly said, "or it wouldn't count as a book at all. Have you written any of it at all yet, Wolf?"

"Of course I have. Lots of it."

"I wish I could read it," Polly said.

"Well, I might have a copy on me. Wait a minute and let me look."

The wolf opened a dilapidated string bag and searched inside it among a sheaf of dog-eared sheets of paper. At last he extracted a small school exercise book with grey paper covers and handed it modestly to Polly.

On the outside of the front cover was printed:

STUDENTS' EXERCISE BOOK

Below this was a space for the name and class of the student. This was filled in: NAME—Wolf. CLASS—Upper.

Polly opened the book and looked inside.

"Once upon a time," she read, "there was a very clever Wolf. He knew a stupid girl called Polly. One day he ate her all up."

A line or two farther down the page, the author had tried again.

"Fortunately I was born. My mother and father were wolves, so naturally I was one too. I am clever, though some people call me stupid which I am not, only they are so stupid themselves they can't see I am the Clever one. One day I caught Polly and ate her up."

Over the page was a third attempt.

"It was a lovely day," the wolf had written, "and the Clever Wolf went out for a walk. Suddenly he saw poor stupid little Polly, so he jumped on her and ate. . . ."

Here the masterpiece abruptly ended. The rest of the book was empty.

"What do you think of it?" the wolf asked eagerly.

The Clever Wolf and Poor Stupid Little Polly (II)

"Well," Polly said kindly. "I think it's very good as far as you've got. But it's not very far, is it? I mean there's got to be a bit more than that to make a proper book, hasn't there?"

"You mean the stories aren't long enough?"

"No, I don't think they are. They seem somehow—well, like you said, they haven't any middles."

"I know," the wolf said, in despair, "but what can I do about it? You see my wolf is so clever, he catches Polly at once and eats her up. There's none of this TALK that goes on in that other book," the wolf said scornfully, "why, talk is all they ever do. Quite different from me. So when I'm writing about it they don't talk, they just do things, and what I do, in my book, is, I eat you up."

"Yes, I see," Polly agreed. "Only it doesn't make such a good story."

"It's a wonderful story!"

"All right, it's a wonderful story—for you, at any rate. But it isn't long enough."

"It will be if I write some more of them."

"You can't."

"Yes I can, easily. I wrote those three without any difficulty——"

"But you can't put all those three into your book."

"Why not?"

"Oh you Stupid Wolf!" Polly cried, exasperated. "How can you have three stories, one after another, about us, if you've eaten me up in the first one? Where am I supposed to come from in the second and the third, if I'm inside you before they ever begin?"

"Oh," the wolf said. "Funny, I never thought of that. And they were such good stories, too," he added sadly. "Never mind," he said suddenly, "I always said all this talk won't get us anywhere."

He looked hastily up and down the street. There was no one about. The wolf turned and pounced on Polly.

But it wasn't on Polly. She had opened the door of the bookshop and slipped inside. Just in time. Through the window, the infuriated wolf saw her speak to the proprietor, who went away to the back of the shop and came back with a heavy looking volume.

With hardly a glance at the window, Polly propped the book up on a shelf so that the wolf could see its title, as she began to read.

How to Deal, the title read, *With Dumb Animals*.

Father Christmas

———————

One day Polly was in the kitchen, washing currants and sultanas to put in a birthday cake, when the front door bell rang.

"Oh dear," said Polly's mother, "my hands are all floury. Be a kind girl, Polly, and go and open the door for me, will you?"

Polly was a kind girl, and she dried her hands and went to the front door. As she left the kitchen, her mother called after her.

"But don't open the door if it's a wolf!"

This reminded Polly of some of her earlier adventures, and before she opened the door, she said cautiously, through the letter box, "Who are you?"

"A friend," said a familiar voice.

"Which one?" Polly asked. "Mary?"

"No, not Mary."

"Jennifer?"

"No, not Jennifer."

"Penelope?"

"No. At least I don't think so. No," said the wolf decidedly, "not Penelope."

"Well, I don't know who you are then," Polly said. "I can't guess. You tell me."

"Father Christmas."

"*Father Christmas*?" said Polly. She was so much surprised that she nearly opened the front door by mistake.

"Father Christmas," said the person on the doorstep. "With a sack full of toys. Now be a good little girl, Polly, and open the door and I'll give you a present out of my sack."

Polly didn't answer at once.

"Did you say Father Christmas?" she asked at last.

"Yes of course I did," said the wolf loudly. "Surely you've heard of Father Christmas before, haven't you? Comes to good children and gives them presents and all that. But not, of course, to naughty little girls who don't open doors when they're told to."

"Yes," Polly said.

"Well, then, what's wrong with that? You know all about Father Christmas and I'm pretending to be—I mean, here he is. I don't see what's bothering you and making you so slow."

"I've heard of Father Christmas, of course," Polly agreed. "But not in the middle of the summer."

"Middle of the what?" the wolf shouted through the door.

"Middle of the summer."

There was a short silence.

"How do you know it's the summer?" the wolf asked argumentatively.

"We're making Mother's birthday cake."

"Well? I don't see what that has to do with it."

"Mother's birthday is in July."

"Perhaps she's rather late in making her cake?" the wolf suggested.

"No, she isn't. She's a few days early, as a matter of fact."

"You mean it's going to be her birthday in a day or two?"

"You've got it, Wolf," Polly agreed.

"So we're in July now?"

"Yes."

"It's not Christmas?"

"No."

"Not even if we happened to be in Australia? They have Christmas in the summer there, you know," the wolf said persuasively.

"But not here. It's nearly half a year till Christmas," Polly said firmly.

Father Christmas

"A pity," the wolf said, "I really thought I'd got you that time. I must have muddled up my calendar again—it's so confusing, all the weeks starting with Mondays."

Polly heard the would-be Father Christmas clumping down the path from the front door; she went back to the currants.

The weeks went by; Mother's birthday was over and forgotten, holidays by the sea marked the end of summer and the beginning of autumn, and it was not until the end of September, when the leaves were turning yellow and brown, and the days were getting shorter and colder, that Polly heard from the wolf again. She was in the sitting-room when the telephone bell rang; Polly lifted the receiver.

"I ont oo thpeak oo Folly," a very muffled voice said.

"I'm sorry," Polly said, politely, "I really can't hear."

"Thpeak oo FOlly."

"I still can't quite hear," Polly said.

"I ont oo—oh BOTHER these beastly whiskers," said quite a different voice. "There, now can you hear? I've taken bits of them off."

"Yes, I can hear all right," Polly said puzzled. "But how can you take off your whiskers?"

"They weren't really mine. I mean they're mine, of course, but not in the usual way. I didn't grow them, I bought them."

"Well," Polly asked, "how did you keep them on before you took them off?"

"Stuck them on with gum," the voice replied cheerfully. "But I haven't taken that bit off yet. The bit I took off was the bit that goes all round your mouth. You know, a moustache. It got awfully in the way of talking, though. The hair kept on getting into my mouth."

"It sounded rather funny," Polly agreed. "But why did you have to put it on?"

"So as to look like the real one."

"The real what?"

"Father Christmas, of course, silly. How would I be able to make you think I was Father Christmas if I didn't wear a white beard and all that cotton woolly sort of stuff round my face, and a red coat and hood and all that?"

"Wolf," said Polly solemnly—for of course it couldn't be anyone else.—"Do you mean to say you were pretending to be Father Christmas?"

"Yes."

"And then what?"

"I was going to say if you'd meet me at some lonely spot—say the cross roads at midnight—I'd give you a present out of my sack."

"And you thought I'd come?"

"Well," said the wolf persuasively, "after all I look exactly like Santa Claus now."

"Yes, but I can't see you."

"Can't See Me?" said the wolf, in surprise.

"We can't either of us see each other. You try, Wolf."

There was a long silence. Polly rattled the receiver.

"Wolf!" she called. "Wolf, are you there?"

"Yes," said the wolf's voice, at last.

"What are you doing?"

"Well, I was having a look. I tried with a small telescope I happened to have by me, but I must admit I can't see much. The trouble is that it's so terribly dark in there. Hold on for a minute, Polly. I'm just going to fetch a candle."

Polly held on. Presently, she heard a fizz and a splutter as the match was struck to light the candle. There was a long pause, broken by the wolf's heavy breathing. Polly heard him muttering: "Not down there. . . . Try the other end then. . . . Perhaps if I unscrew this bit. . . . Let's see this bit of wire properly. . . ."

There was a deafening explosion, which made poor Polly jump. Her ear felt as if it would never hear properly again. Obviously the wolf had held his candle too near to the wires and something had exploded.

"I do hope he hasn't hurt himself," Polly thought, as she hung up her own receiver. "It sounded like an awfully loud explosion."

She saw the wolf a day or two later in the street. His face

and head were covered with bandages, from amongst which one eye looked sadly out.

"Oh Wolf, I am so sorry," said kind Polly, stopping as he was just going to pass her. "Does it hurt very much? It must have been an awfully big explosion."

"Explosion? Where?" said the wolf, looking eagerly up and down the street.

"Not here. At your home. When you rang me up the other day."

"Oh that!" said the wolf airily. "That wasn't really an explosion. Just a spark or two and a sort of bang, that's all. I just got the candle in the way of the wires and they melted together, or something. Nothing to get alarmed about, thank you, Polly."

"But your face," Polly said, "the bandages. Didn't you get hurt in that explosion?"

"No. But that gum! Whee-e-e-w! I'll tell you what, Polly," the wolf said impressively. "Don't ever try and stick a beard or whiskers on top of where your fur grows, with spirit gum. It goes on all right, but getting it off is—well! If it had been my own hair it couldn't have been more painful getting it off. Next time I'm going to have one of those beards on sort of spectacle things you just hook over your ears. Don't you think that would be better?"

"Much better."

"Not so painful to take off?"

"I should think not," Polly agreed.

"Well you just wait till I've got these bandages off," the wolf said gaily, "and then you'll see! My own mother wouldn't know me."

Perhaps it took longer than Polly expected to grow wolf

fur again: at any rate it was a month or two before Polly heard from the wolf again, and she had nearly forgotten his promise, or threat, of coming to find her. It was just before Christmas, and Polly was out with her mother doing Christmas shopping. The streets were crowded and the shop windows were gay with silver balls and frosted snow. Everything sparkled and shone and glowed, and Polly held on to Mother's hand and danced along the pavements.

"Polly," said her mother. "Would you like to go to the toy department of Jarold's? I've got to get one or two small things there, and you could look round. I think they've got some displays of model railways and puppets, and they generally have a sort of Christmas fair with Father Christmas to talk to."

Polly said yes, she would very much, and they turned in at the doors of the enormous shop and took a luxuriant gilded lift up to the third floor, to the toy department. It really was fascinating. While her mother was buying coloured glass balls for the Christmas tree, and a snowstorm for Lucy, Polly wandered about and looked at everything. She saw trains and dolls and bears; she saw puzzles and puppets and paperweights. She saw bicycles, tricycles, swings and slides, boats and boomerangs and cars and carriages. At last she saw an archway, above which was written "Christmas Tree Land". Polly walked in.

There was a sort of scene arranged in the shop itself, and it was very pretty. There were lots of Christmas trees, all covered with sparkling white snow, and the rest of the place was rather dark so that all the light seemed to come from the trees. In the distance you could see reindeer grazing, or running, and high snowy mountains and forests of more Christmas trees. At the end of the part where Polly was, sat Father Christmas on a sort of throne. There was a crowd of children round him and a man in ordinary clothes, a shop manager, was encouraging their mothers to bring them up to Father Christmas so that they could tell him what they hoped to find in their stockings or under the tree on Christmas Day.

Polly drew near. She thought she would tell Father Christmas that what she wanted more than anything else in the world was a clown's suit. She joined a line of children waiting to get up to the throne.

The child in front of Polly was frightened. She kept on running out of line back to her mother, and her mother kept on putting her back in her place again.

"I don't want to go and talk to that Father Christmas," the little girl said, "he isn't a proper Father Christmas."

"Nonsense," her mother said sharply. "Don't be so silly. Stand in that line and go up and tell him what you want in your stocking like a nice little girl."

The little girl began to cry. Polly, looking sharply at Father Christmas couldn't help rather agreeing with her. Father Christmas had the usual red coat and hood and a lot of bushy white hair all over his face. But somehow his manner wasn't quite right. He certainly asked the children questions, but not in the pleasantest tone of voice, and his reply to some of their answers was more of a snarl than a promise.

The little girl in front of Polly was finally persuaded to go up and say something in a breathy, awestruck whisper. Polly, just behind her, was near enough to hear the answer.

"Box of sweets," said Father Christmas in a distinctly unpleasant tone. "What do you want a box of sweets for?

You're quite fat enough already to satisfy any ordinary person, I should think."

The child clutched her mother's hand tightly, and the manager who was standing near, looked displeased. "Come, come," Polly heard him say sharply in Father Christmas's ear, "you can do better than that, surely."

Father Christmas jumped, threw a sharp glance over his shoulder at the manager and leant forward to the little girl. "Yes, of course you shall have a box of sweets," he said. "Only wouldn't you like something more interesting? For instance a big juicy steak, with plenty of fried potatoes? Or what about pork chops? I always think myself there's nothing like. . . ."

"Next please," the manager called out loudly. "And a happy Christmas to you, dear," he added to the surprised little girl who was being led away by her mother, unable to make head or tail of this extraordinary Father Christmas.

Polly moved up. The Father Christmas inclined his ear towards her to hear what she wanted in her stocking, but Polly had something else to say.

"Wolf, how could you!" she hissed in a horrified whisper. "Pretending to be Father Christmas to all these poor little children—and you're not doing it at all well, either."

"It wasn't my fault," the wolf said, gloomily. "I never meant to let myself in for this terrible affair. I just put on my costume—and I did the beard rather well this time, don't you think?—and I went out to see if I could find you, and this wretched man"—he threw a glance of black hate at the shop manager—"nobbled me in the street, and pulled me in here, and set me to asking the same stupid question of all these beastly children. And they all want the same things," he added venomously. "If it's boys they want space guns, and if it's girls they want party frocks and television sets. Not one of them's asked for anything sensible to eat. One of them did ask for a baby sister," he said thoughtfully, "but did she really want her to eat, I ask myself?"

"I should hope not," Polly said firmly.

"And I'm much too hot and my whiskers tickle my ears horribly," the wolf complained. "And there's not a chance of snatching a bite with this man standing over me all the time."

"Wolf, you wouldn't eat the children!" Polly said in protest.

"Not all of them," the wolf answered. "Some of them aren't very——"

"Next please," said the manager loudly. A deliciously plump juicy little boy was pushed to stand just behind Polly. He was reciting to himself and his mother, "I want a gun, an' I want soldiers, an' I want a rocking 'orse, an' I want a steam engine, an' I want. . . ."

"I think you're going to be busy today," Polly said, "I probably shan't be seeing you for a time. Happy Christmas," she added politely, as she made way for the juicy little boy. "I hope you enjoy yourself with all these friendly little girls and boys."

"Grrrrrr," replied Father Christmas. "I'll enjoy myself still more when I've unhooked my beard and got my teeth into one unfriendly little girl. Just you wait, Polly: Christmas or no Christmas, I'll get you yet."

The Hypnotist

Polly was sitting on a bench on the Heath near one of the ponds, looking at the boys sailing boats. There were a good many people, sitting, standing, and talking to each other, so Polly was not really frightened, though she was a little surprised, to find the wolf sitting at the other end of the bench from her. When she saw him he was gazing at her fixedly.

"Good morning, Wolf," Polly said, politely.

"Good morning, Polly," the wolf said, in a deeper voice than usual.

"It's a lovely day."

"Yes," said the wolf, without taking his eyes off Polly's face.

"Don't you like seeing the ships sailing on the pond?"

"Yes," said the wolf, without casting an eye in their direction.

"Especially the sailing ships—the ones with sails."

"Especially the ones with tails. . . . Oh do be quiet, Polly," the wolf said impatiently in his ordinary voice. "How can I concentrate when you keep on talking about things that don't matter?"

"I'm sorry," said Polly, a little hurt in her feelings. "I was only trying to be polite. I didn't know you were concentrating."

She turned back to look at the pond again, leaving the wolf to his concentration. But this time he interrupted her.

"Polly," said the wolf in his new deep voice, "look at me."

Polly turned and looked at him.

"Look at me," the wolf said again.

"I am looking," Polly said impatiently. "What is it? I can't see anything different."

"Look at me," said the wolf for the third time.

Polly looked very carefully. Then she clapped her hands.

"I see! How silly of me not to notice before. You've painted a white moustache over your mouth like a funny man in a pantomime. It's very good, Wolf."

"I haven't," said the wolf crossly. "Bother those ice-cream cornets! They always get all over you." He put out a long wet red tongue and licked the moustache off. "Better?"

"A little more to the left."

"Thanks," said the wolf, and then, going back to his deep voice, he began again. "Look at me, Polly."

"I'm looking," said Polly.

"Look at me, Polly."

"I'm still looking."

"Look at me Polly."

"I know!" Polly said, suddenly enlightened. She continued to stare at the wolf, without saying any more. Presently she winked, then she made a face, then she wiggled her scalp. At almost the same moment a fly, who had been buzzing round for some time, alighted on one of the wolf's ears. Immediately both ears stood upright, twitched violently, and the wolf shook his head with something between a sneeze and a hiccup.

Polly burst out laughing.

"You win," she said as soon as she could, "I can only wiggle the top of my head, but your ears are splendid. Let's try again. Why what's the matter, Wolf?"

For the wolf, not looking at all pleased with his triumph, was tapping the ground angrily with his paw and scowling in her direction.

"What do you think we're doing, may I ask?" he demanded.

"Playing who can laugh last. Aren't we?" Polly asked, puzzled. "Why did you keep on telling me to look at you, like that, if we aren't? And I laughed first, so you've won, and you needn't look so annoyed about it."

The Hypnotist

"I wasn't playing anything so childish," the wolf said, angrily. "I shouldn't dream of partaking in such an infantile pastime. You don't seem to realize, Polly, I'm giving you a chance of sharing a very interesting scientific experiment."

"What's that?"

"Trying out something new. Scientific. Science. You know." The wolf waved his arms about to demonstrate science. "Steam engines, and wheels go round, and bombs, and what makes guinea pigs have no tails and that sort of thing."

"Oh," said Polly, "but what has that to do with me?"

"Well, I want you to do an experiment with me."

"But I don't know anything about steam engines," Polly said, "or bombs. And not much about guinea pigs," she added.

"It's not about any of those, silly. It's something much newer. It's very fashionable, in fact. Have you ever heard of Hypnosis?"

"Is it a horse?" asked Polly. Her sister was interested in horses and Polly had heard many of their names.

"It's certainly not a horse. It's a—well it's a sort of a thing. I'll explain. Some doctors can do what's called hypnotize other people—it's like putting them to sleep, so they don't know what they're doing, and then the other person, the doctor who is doing the hypnotizing, can tell the person who's asleep what to do, and she has to do it."

"It's rather muddling," Polly remarked.

"No it isn't," the wolf said angrily. "It's perfectly simple. Look, I hypnotize you and you sort of go to sleep and I tell you to go and walk into the pond and you have to."

"I should say 'no'," Polly protested.

"You can't. You're asleep."

"But if I'm asleep why do I hear what you say?"

"Because you're hypnotized. And when you're hypnotized you have to do whatever the hypnotist tells you, whether you like it or not. And now I'm going to hypnotize you," the wolf said abruptly, and then in his deep voice, "look at me, Polly."

"I'd rather look at the pond. I don't think I want to be hypnotized, Wolf."

"Look at me, Polly."

"There's a ship with red sails. I do like red sails. I like them much better than white."

"Look at me, Polly."

"Oh all right," Polly said, impatiently, "I'll look if you want me to. Only do hurry up, and tell me when it's over."

"Look at me, Polly—and don't talk," the wolf added in his natural voice.

For several moments the wolf and Polly sat staring at each other from opposite ends of the bench. Neither of them moved and neither spoke.

"You are feeling very sleepy, Polly!" said the wolf.

"Yes, I am, rather," Polly agreed. "I think it's the sun. It's really warm today—I expect it's almost spring."

"You are feeling very sleepy, Polly," said the wolf again.

Polly did not answer.

"You are asleep, Polly," the wolf said, his voice deeper than ever.

"Almost," Polly said, comfortably. She shut her eyes.

"Now you are asleep," the wolf said, leaning forward

towards her. "You have to do everything I tell you. You won't wake up till I tell you to. Now, listen carefully. Are you listening?"

There was a short silence.

"Are you listening?" the wolf said, impatiently.

Polly nodded, sleepily.

"Good. Now Polly, after I've woken you up out of your hypnotic sleep, you are going to get up and walk down the road on the right, across the next little bit of heath until you come to the house on the corner where the two big elm trees have grown through the old wall. You turn along there and you go on till you come to the house with the green door and the shiny brass knocker, and you go in. That's my house, Polly. The door won't be locked and you just walk in, straight through the hall and into the kitchen at the end and —well I'll meet you there."

The wolf's voice died away into a loving whisper. Polly opened one eye.

"And then what happens, Wolf?"

"And then I eat you all up. Oh yes—I forgot to mention one thing—there won't be any talk."

"No talk at all?"

"Not a word. You just come in and I cook you and eat you up and there's no argument. None of this 'Wouldn't you rather have this, Wolf?' or 'Do you think we'd better wait for a day or two?' or anything like that. Do you understand, Polly?"

"I understand, Wolf."

"Very well. Now, Polly," said the wolf, in an artificially cheerful voice, "in a minute's time from now you are going to wake up. You will feel very much refreshed, as if you had

had eight hours of sound sleep. And after you've woken up you're going to do what I told you."

"I'm awfully sleepy," Polly said, stretching her arms and blinking at the sun.

"But refreshed?"

"I don't notice it much yet," Polly admitted. She stood up and started walking away from the pond.

"Hi!" the wolf called after her, "that's not the right direction. I said down the road on the right."

"I know," said Polly. "But I think something must have gone wrong with the experiment. I heard everything you said, but I just don't want to do it. I don't feel any more like walking into your house and getting eaten up than I ever do."

"Didn't you fall into a trance? Weren't you properly asleep?"

"I'm afraid not," Polly said apologetically.

"Bother, bother, Bother, BOTHER," said the wolf, "nothing ever goes right. And I'm sure I did all the things it said in the book! Wait a minute, let me think."

He sank his head between his paws and shut his eyes, concentrating. Polly began to move further away.

"Don't go," the wolf pleaded, "wait just a second, Polly, I've remembered something. You have to look at a bright light till your eyes get tired and then we can start all the suggesting part of it."

Polly looked quickly around her. As lunch time approached the crowd had thinned out, and there were now only a few people left round the pond. It would not be very funny, Polly reflected, to be left quite alone with a hungry wolf, whether he succeeded in hypnotizing her or not.

"Please, Polly," pleaded the wolf. "Just look at the sun for a minute or two and see if you don't begin to feel sleepy and hypnotized."

"It's very bad for you to look at the sun," Polly protested. "My father says you can hurt your eyes very badly if you look straight at the sun for even a short time."

"Pooh," said the wolf, "that may be true of poor weak human eyes, but we wolves can look at the sun for hours without it hurting us."

To prove his point he gazed straight into the sun.

"Be careful, Wolf," said Polly kindly after a short time, "don't go and blind yourself just to prove that your eyes are stronger than mine."

"Your eyes are stronger than mine," the wolf repeated in a far away sing-song voice.

"Wolf! Do listen properly! I said, don't be silly, stop

looking at the sun and go home before you hurt yourself."

"Don't be silly," the wolf said, still in his faraway voice. "Stop looking at the sun." He withdrew his eyes from the sky and fixed them on Polly, but obviously without seeing her at all. "Go home before I hurt myself."

He got up off the seat and began to walk in the direction of his house, but without taking any notice of where he was going. In another minute he would have walked straight into the pond, if Polly hadn't caught him and guided him away from it.

"Wolf! What is the matter with you? Are you asleep or something?"

"Asleep or something," the wolf said, nodding his head drowsily.

"Oh Wolf!" Polly cried, "I see! You're the one who got hypnotized, because you would insist on looking at the sun. All right, now I'll tell you what to do. Go home, Wolf, and have a nice vegetarian lunch—some biscuits and cheese and a lightly boiled egg. And then go to bed and have a long long sleep and when you wake up you'll feel very much refreshed and very obliging and not at all hungry. And don't ever come and try to eat me all up again, do you understand? Never, never, never."

"Never," repeated the wolf, and he sounded so sad that Polly, who really quite enjoyed having a wolf around to get the better of, said relentingly:

"Well, not for a long time. And I'm clever, and you're stupid, remember that!"

"I'm clever and you're stupid," repeated the wolf dreamily as he took his way off, leaving Clever Polly wondering what sort of a wolf she would meet next time.

The Deaf Wolf

"It's a good idea," the wolf said to himself, putting down the book of English fairy stories he had just been reading. "It's very difficult getting Polly within snapping distance. It's worth trying, anyway."

He looked again at the illustration of a fox with one paw behind his ear, pretending to be so deaf that the incautious gingerbread man talking to him would come nearer in order to make him hear.

"I could do that easily," the wolf thought. "I'll put cotton wool in my ears. Then I really shan't be able to hear anything Polly says, and she'll come right up to shout in my ear and I'll just give one spring, like it says in the book and——"

He lost himself in a happy dream.

*   *   *

Polly was in the garden, playing with Lucy. First Lucy wanted to swing: then she wanted to play ball: then she wanted to pick all her mother's precious roses, and Polly could only divert her attention from this scheme by offering to give her rides on her back. She was on all fours, getting her knees and the skirt of her frock very green on the grass, and being half throttled by Lucy's plump arms round her neck, when she heard a curious noise on the other side of the hedge.

"A-harrup—a-harrup—a-harrup," the noise said.

"Horse!" said Lucy delightedly. She slid off Polly's back and went to look through a special hole in the hedge, just the right height for her, which she had discovered a week or so ago.

"It didn't sound like a horse," Polly said, getting up and stretching her cramped legs deliciously.

"Not horse," Lucy agreed. "No horse," she added, rather disappointed as she still saw nothing in the road outside. "Polly horse again?" she asked persuasively.

"No, Lucy, I really can't," Polly said. "I'm too tired."

"Lucy tired," said Lucy, lying down full length on the grass to make sure she was understood.

"All right. Let's both be tired," said Polly, thankfully lying down beside her.

"I not tired," Lucy said indignantly, getting up again immediately. "Sing Oranges and Lemons."

"A-harrack!" said a persistent voice beyond the hedge. A familiar black head rose above it and looked over into the garden.

"Dog! Big dog!" said Lucy, delighted.

"Good morning, Wolf," said Polly, politely.

"Not as much as yesterday," the Wolf said in a gloomy voice.

"I don't quite understand," Polly said. "I didn't ask you about yesterday."

"But a bit more than the day before. It was one of those chops with nothing but gristle and bone," the wolf explained.

The Deaf Wolf

"I don't know what you thought I said," Polly shouted across the hedge, "but I wasn't talking about chops. I just said good morning."

"And I'm warning you, if you're talking about warning," the wolf said, suddenly disagreeable. "I'll get you sooner or later as sure as eggs is eggs."

"Are eggs. Not is eggs, it's not grammar. Are eggs."

"However many legs you have," the wolf said nastily.

There was a pause. It seemed a difficult conversation to keep up, and Polly was not sure where they had got to. Lucy, who had stopped trying to be the chopper as well as the chorus in Oranges and Lemons, had come to stand beside her to stare up at the wolf, her hands behind her back, stomach well out. It seemed a good moment to introduce her.

"This is Lucy, my smallest sister," she said.

"I'm sorry," the wolf said, more politely. "I hope it doesn't hurt."

"What doesn't hurt? Lucy doesn't, only when she rides on my back for too long at a time."

"It's a funny place to have a blister." The wolf looked puzzled. "I always get them on my paws. Perhaps it's the way you walk."

"What's wrong with the way I walk? I can't walk any other way."

"Oh well," the wolf said, huffily, "don't talk then if you don't want to."

"Oh dear," Polly sighed. "You are being difficult today, Wolf. You don't seem to like anything I say, you keep on misunderstanding. You seem to think I'm trying to be rude."

"I don't," the wolf said. "I only wish you'd try a bit harder."

"Try to be rude?"

"Yes. If you'd try to be food I could easily pretend you were, and then—well you would be," the wolf said simply.

"Oh you're hopeless!" Polly said angrily. "Why don't you listen properly? I said Rude, RUDE, not Food."

"Very impolite of you," the wolf replied. "I never have cared for rude children!"

"Big, big, BIG dog!" Lucy said admiringly.

"I am not!" the wolf said, hotly. "Many names I've been called before now, but Pig Hog never. You've taught this horrid little girl, whoever she is, to be as rude as you are, Polly, and you ought to be ashamed of yourself."

Lucy, not liking to be looked at so angrily, turned round and ran back into the house to find her mother and ask if

The Deaf Wolf

lunch wasn't nearly ready. The wolf looked after her thoughtfully, noticing the twinkling of her plump legs, and a pleasanter expression came over his face.

"She seems quite at home in your house, Polly. Staying with you for a time, perhaps? A relation? Cousin or something? Never mind," he added hastily, as Polly opened her mouth to answer, "I don't really want to know. She might be your sister for all I care. What is important now we are alone at last, is to get on with our conversation."

"We hadn't got very far," Polly said. "You didn't seem to hear anything I said."

"Instead of what?"

"I SAID!" Polly shouted, "NOT INSTEAD! I SAID!"

"What did you say?"

"I said you didn't seem to hear what I said."

"Oh," the wolf said looking interested. "And what did you say?"

Polly found this difficult to answer. "A lot of things," she said at last, unable to remember any one of them. Her throat was quite dry with talking so loudly across the hedge, but it was only when she really shouted that the wolf seemed to hear properly.

"I see," she said suddenly, in her ordinary voice again, "you're deaf! How awful for you. I am sorry!"

"I know you're Polly," the wolf said. "You don't have to tell me that at this time of day."

"I said I was SORRY."

"It's all right," the wolf said amiably, "you can't help it. Anyhow as Pollies go you're quite all right."

"You're DEAF, Wolf!" Polly shouted.

"Yes!" said the wolf looking really delighted, "you're quite

44

right, I am. Clever of you to notice. Now let's get started."

The wolf trotted down the road till he was opposite the garden gate, lay down and turned his eyes on her in a rather theatrical way. Then he panted slightly with his tongue out, and waited.

Polly waited too.

Presently the wolf got up, shook himself, came a yard or two nearer the gate and lay down again in almost exactly the same position. He again turned his eyes towards Polly, and waited.

Polly waited too.

The wolf switched his tail angrily about, raising a good deal of dust out of the road; then he shook his head violently and scratched at his ears. Two small objects fell out of them, which he covered with his paw. Then he looked even more intently at Polly.

Polly looked back at the wolf.

"Well, go on," the wolf said at last impatiently. "Aren't you ever going to begin?"

"Begin what?"

"Talking to me, of course. Telling me things I can't hear properly."

"But if you can't hear properly, what's the good," Polly began, but the wolf cut her short.

"Go on, go on! It doesn't matter what it's about, only do, for goodness' sake, talk!"

"About anything? Doesn't it matter at all?"

"Anything," the wolf said, eagerly, "absolutely anything. Just go on talking, Polly, and I promise I won't complain. I just want to hear your voice, and I'll be quite content—or rather I just want not to hear your voice."

"I don't understand," Polly said.

"Never mind. You don't have to understand. You only have to talk."

"And you're not deaf now. You can hear everything I say."

"Of course!" cried the wolf delighted, "that's what's wrong! How stu— I mean that wasn't as clever of me as usual. I quite forgot I was *hearing* you. That won't do at all."

He picked up from the road the two objects which had fallen when he scratched his ears, and tucked them back, one in each ear.

"Ear plugs," he explained to the wondering Polly. "Now I'm all right. Shan't be able to hear a word you say. Now, talk."

Still without understanding, Polly began.

"Hoddley, poddley, puddle and frogs,

"Cats are to marry the poodle dogs."

She stopped and looked at the wolf to see how he was taking it. He nodded at her agreeably.

"Delightful. I couldn't catch every word, but do go on."

"Cats in blue jackets," continued Polly, "And dogs in red hats,

What will become of the mice and the rats?"

The wolf looked puzzled.

"I don't think I can have heard every word correctly," he said. "It seems an unusual situation. But do go on."

"There isn't any more," said Polly.

"If I'd heard it before I shouldn't ask you to repeat it to me," said the wolf, with a flash of temper.

"THERE ISN'T ANY MORE!" shouted Polly.

The wolf propped himself up elaborately on three legs and put the fourth behind his ear.

"I can't quite catch what you said."

"THERE-ISN'T-ANY-MORE."

"Come a little nearer, my dear," said the wolf, in an un-
naturally sweet voice, "and let me hear what you say."

Polly looked. There was a reasonable distance between the
wolf and herself, but she didn't feel inclined to get very much
nearer. She also had a strong feeling that the wolf had in fact
heard her last shout, which had been a remarkably loud noise.

"WAIT A MOMENT," she called, "I'LL BE BACK AT
ONCE."

She ran into the house. It really was lunch time now, and
Polly was hungry, and the smell coming up from the kitchen
was almost more than she could bear. However she ran up-
stairs to the dressing-up chest on the landing, which con-
tained, among a great many other things, an ear trumpet
which belonged to Mother's great aunt Anna, and had never
been used since she died years and years and years ago.

The Deaf Wolf

It was only a moment before Polly was back in the garden: from well on her side of the gate she offered the ear trumpet to the astonished wolf.

"Just put that to your ear and you'll be able to hear quite well," she said.

"?" said the wolf.

"JUST TAKE THIS AND YOU'LL BE ABLE TO HEAR."

"What is it?" the wolf asked, suspiciously. "Will it go off bang?"

"No, silly. It's for you. It's an ear-trumpet."

"I don't like junket," the wolf said, sulkily.

"AN EAR-TRUMPET! TRY IT."

The wolf put out his paw and took it gingerly. He looked down the big end of the trumpet, and shook his head. Then he squinted through the small end up at the sky. He looked across at Polly.

"PUT YOUR EAR TO IT," she shouted.

"What for?" asked the wolf, shaking the ear trumpet as if he expected something to fall out of it.

"SO THAT YOU CAN HEAR ME TALK."

"But you Stupid little girl," the wolf said, throwing the trumpet back into the garden. "Can't you understand, I don't want to hear you talk? I want Not to be able to hear you talk. I just want you to come closer and closer, until you're so close that I just jump on you and gobble you all up. Now do you understand?"

Polly put the ear-trumpet to her mouth and shouted at the wolf, "TAKE OUT THOSE EARPLUGS FOR A MINUTE, WOLF."

The wolf looked very angry, but he did as Polly asked.

The Deaf Wolf

"Thank goodness for that," Polly said, in her ordinary voice. "I couldn't go on shouting any longer. Look, Wolf, if that's how you'd planned to catch me this time you'd got something quite wrong. Of course I wasn't going to come any nearer."

"Why not?" said the wolf in an aggrieved tone.

"You'd forgotten something. In those stories where the animal—it's usually a fox, isn't it?—pretends to be deaf, the creature he is going to catch comes right up to tell him something. But you got that wrong, Wolf. The creature in the stories always wants to show off. He really wants the fox to hear. But I don't care tuppence if you hear what I'm saying or not. So of course I shan't come any nearer. As a matter of fact there's only one thing I want at the moment and it's nothing to do with your hearing me or not."

"What is it?"

"Lunch," said Polly, tucking the ear-trumpet under her arm and turning towards the house. "And I'm going to have it."

"So do I want mine," said the wolf sadly, turning in the opposite direction, "but it looks as if I wasn't going to have it, today at any rate."

Cherry Stones

———◆◆◆◆◆◆◆◆◆———

It was the middle of the summer, and Polly was having a delicious time one hot, lazy afternoon, sitting in the garden with a bowl of cherries beside her. Beside the patch of grass where she was sitting was a big flat flagstone, which was part of a path, and on this Polly arranged her nicely-sucked-clean cherry stones. She arranged them in different patterns; squares and triangles and a big circle and a star: she rearranged them to write letters with. There were quite a lot of them, and more every minute.

Presently Polly arranged the stones in neat rows of eights. There were several rows. She seemed to be playing some sort of game with them, counting them perhaps: but she didn't look very much pleased with the result. Several times she went through them, a finger hovering for a moment over each stone, and each time she ended by frowning and shaking her head and hastily eating another cherry and adding the stone to her collection. But still she didn't seem satisfied.

The wolf, who had been watching this ritual going on for some time, from the other side of the garden wall, was completely puzzled. He stood it for as long as he could, and then his curiosity got the better of him.

"Hi, Polly!" he said.

Polly jumped. Then she saw the wolf, waved to him, shook her head with her finger to her lips, and went on counting.

"What are you doing, Polly?" the wolf asked.

"Wait a minute," Polly said, "I'm just finishing . . . cotton, rags, silk, satin—oh bother!"

"Why 'Oh bother'?"

"Because it's come wrong again."

"What has?"

"Who I'm going to marry."

The wolf peered a little further over the hedge but saw nothing more than the rows of stones on the path which Polly had been counting before he interrupted her.

"Who you're going to marry?" repeated the wolf.

"And what in. And what I'm going to wear."

"What are you going to wear? And what in?"

"What I go to be married in. Oh you know, Wolf. Coach, carriage, wheelbarrow, dustcart, and I keep on getting wheelbarrow. It's so undignified."

"Where's the wheelbarrow?" said the wolf looking round the garden. "And anyhow aren't you a bit young to be married, Polly? We shall miss you," he added politely.

"Oh dear," Polly sighed. "You are stupid sometimes, Wolf. I'm not going to be married yet, not for ages, but I'm finding out what it will be like by telling on cherry stones. You know, you lay out all your cherry stones and you say a sort of rhyme to yourself and you count the cherry stones as you go, and whatever one you end on is what you're going to get. Like this:

> *Tinker, tailor,*
> *Soldier, sailor,*
> *Rich man, poor man,*
> *Beggarman, thief."*

"Are they all about marriage and weddings?" the wolf inquired.

"All the ones I know are," Polly said, firmly.

"Pooh!" cried the wolf, "we have much more interesting rhymes than that."

"Oh, do you have them too?" Polly said, interested.

"Of course we do. Only we don't generally do them on cherry stones."

"Oh! What do you do them on?"

"Bones," said the wolf simply.

"Ugh! How horrible!" Polly said, and shivered.

"Not at all. There's nothing so comforting as a nice clean bone, well licked by all the members of the family."

"And the rhymes?" asked Polly quickly. "I'd awfully like to hear them, and I'm sure you could think of them if you tried very hard. Have some cherries to help."

She threw him a double handful of cherries. The wolf caught them dextrously in his mouth and ate them, arranging the stones on the road outside the garden out of Polly's sight. Polly heard him murmuring to himself over them and soon his head reappeared over the hedge.

"I've got one of them," he announced.

"Oh, do tell me."

The wolf shut his eyes and recited:

> "*Thinny, Fatty,*
> *In a meat patty*
> *Tender, tough,*
> *It cuts up rough.*"

"I don't think I'd like my husband to be in a meat patty," Polly said, rather puzzled.

"There's another version of that one which some people prefer," the wolf went on, not taking any notice of her remark. "It says:

> '*Juicy,*
> *Tender,*
> *Stringy, tough,*
> *Leathery,*
> *Hairy,*
> *I've had enough.*'

or some people say, 'You've had enough,' but I think that's rather rude."

"I think it's disgusting either way," Polly said. "Who wants a juicy husband? or a leathery one? and I'm not sure how hairy," she added thoughtfully.

"Oh you are Stupid!" the wolf cried angrily. "Can't you ever stop thinking about husbands and weddings? Our rhymes aren't silly little jingles about useless things like that, they're proper poetry, about the real things in life. About FOOD," he finished, seeing that Polly still looked bewildered.

"Oh, food," Polly said, understanding at last.

"Give me a few more cherries, Polly," the wolf begged, "and I'll tell you some more."

Polly threw the wolf another handful of cherries and he disappeared behind the hedge once again.

"Bother!" she heard him say to himself, "I must have swallowed one. It isn't coming out right.

"Polly," he said, suddenly reappearing, "could you spare me just one more—? Thank you! Now I shall get it right."

Through the thick dark green leaves of the hedge, Polly heard him mutter:

> "*Young,*
> *Old,*
> *Hot,*
> *Cold.*
> *Nasty,*
> *Nice,*
> *Served up twice.*"

"What did you say, Wolf?" she called out.

"Served up twice. And I don't like the same dish twice running. It puts me off my food. I shall have to have another cherry, please, Polly."

"You haven't told me the rhyme yet, Wolf."

> *"Fought,*
> *Caught,*
> *Stolen,*
> *Bought"*

gabbled the wolf in a great hurry. "My cherry, please."

Polly threw it. She ate another handful herself and began to count the stones on the path again.

> *"Church,*
> *Bar,*
> *Sword,*
> *Squire,*
> *Artist,*
> *Lord."*

"Now this," the wolf announced, leaning cosily over the hedge, "is a really useful one. It's so difficult, isn't it, to know straight off whether a joint of meat is going to be enough for everyone?

> *Plenty for all,*
> *Will just feed four,*
> *Three get a meal,*
> *For two, no more.*
> *Enough for one,*
> *My story's done."*

"And if it's only enough for one, and there's a whole family of you, what do you do?" Polly inquired.

"Don't tell them, of course." The wolf looked amazed, "After all if there's only enough for one, it's very hard on them, isn't it, to know that you had it and they didn't?"

"You might give it to one of them," Polly suggested.

"I should never do anything so silly," the wolf replied roundly.

Polly and the wolf considered each other for a minute or two over the hedge.

"But this time," the wolf said triumphantly, "it all comes out right. It's young, a meal for three (which means a good hearty meal), it's in a meat patty, or soon will be, it's stringy, that's bad, but one can't have everything. And it's stolen, which is just what it's going to be, so NOW, Polly, I'VE GOT YOU," and he jumped over the hedge right into the garden.

"Wait a moment," Polly said, thinking very hard and very quickly, "I must count my cherry stones too."

"Nonsense," the wolf said, "I'm in a hurry. I'm not going to wait even half a moment. I'm going to carry you off and eat you up NOW."

"Oh, Wolf," said Polly, reproachfully, "I don't think you're being very kind. After all I did give you the cherries whose stones you've been counting, and I could have eaten them all myself, you know. It's only fair that I should be allowed to count my stones and see what they say about the situation."

"All that stuff about marriage," the wolf sneered, "I don't see how that is going to help you."

"They aren't all about marriage," Polly said, as firmly as she could. "This one's about food too, like yours, but in a different way. It's about oneself as food—how one tastes. It's very important for a Polly." she said desperately.

"Sounds interesting," the wolf admitted. "What is it?"

"Well I'll tell you," Polly said, "if you'll let me do it on my cherry stones."

"And it will really tell us how you'll taste?"

"It should," Polly answered, hoping fervently that she had worked it out right in her mind.

"We'll do it together," the wolf promised. "Now say it."

"I'm delightful," began Polly.

"I'm delicious.

"I'm ten times better than Jane."

"Excellent," said the wolf, heartily. "I see we shan't go far wrong on that. Let's begin counting."

"I haven't finished," Polly said, quickly. "That's only the first half."

"Oh, is there more? Go on, then."

"I'm as tough as old shoe," Polly went on.

"Even steamed, I won't do.

"I'll give you a terrible pain."

The wolf snarled angrily.

"That's all," said Polly.

"I don't believe a word of it," the wolf said, "you look tender enough. Not a bit like an old shoe."

"It's only the rhyme," Polly reminded him. "I wasn't actually saying it about myself."

The wolf looked more cheerful.

"There are the stones," Polly said, pointing to the flag-stone and hoping desperately that she had counted right while she made up her rhyme.

The wolf lay down on the grass, beside the flag-stone.

"You count them out," he said anxiously to Polly. "The suspense is almost too much for me. I can't wait to know what you're going to be like."

Polly obediently squatted down beside the wolf and pointed to each stone in turn, as she recited her verse.

> "*I'm delightful,*
> *I'm delicious,*
> *I'm ten times better than Jane.*
> *I'm as tough as old shoe,*
> *Even steamed I won't do,*
> *I'll give you a horrible pain.*"

There were a good many cherry stones and Polly went through the rhyme several times. She was getting very nervous and the wolf was getting very impatient before she reached the final count.

"I'm delicious," said Polly trying to see out of the corner of her eye whether there were four or five stones left.

"I'm ten times better than Jane,

I'm as tough as old shoe (there are two more, I hope it isn't three).

"Even steamed I won't do,

"I'll give you a horrible pain (thank goodness it really is the last one)."

"Go on," said the wolf, who had shut his eyes during the last round.

"That's all," said Polly.

"It can't be. There must be some more. Begin again, then."

"There aren't any more stones," Polly explained.

"You mean to stand there, and tell me you'll give me a pain?"

"That's what the cherry stones say," Polly said.

"But when I counted mine they said you'd be young, and in a meat patty and——"

"It doesn't matter how you'd cook me, I'd still give you a pain."

"Enough for three," the wolf moaned.

"That just makes it a worse pain."

"I might do it on my cherry stones. It might come out different," the wolf suggested, suddenly hopeful.

"It wouldn't show you how I'd taste," Polly warned him, but the wolf was already over the further side of the hedge, counting busily. A triumphant roar came from him and his head appeared over the bushes.

"Ten times better than Jane!" he cried. "It's all right, Polly, I can have you."

"Oh Wolf," Polly sighed, "don't be so stupid. What your cherry stones say is just about you, not about me. How *you'll* taste when someone eats you."

"I hadn't thought of that." The wolf hesitated. "Are you sure, Polly?"

"Quite sure. After all it says 'I' all the way through, doesn't it? Not 'You're ten times better than Jane', but I. Meaning you, Wolf, if you're counting. See?"

"I see."

"And," said Polly, following up her advantage, "do your cherry stones really say you're ten times better than Jane?"

"They certainly do," the wolf said, proudly.

"Then look out!" said Polly, taking a step towards him. "Because I don't think, this time, I can resist trying to see if it's true, and I know just what Jane is like."

"Oh!" said the wolf. He didn't look to see if Polly was coming any further after him. He ran as fast as he could down the road in case fierce Polly caught up with him and began to eat him. When at last he dared to slow down and finally to stop, he sat by the roadside, congratulating himself on his narrow escape, and licking the dust off his tail.

"At any rate," he thought. "It was lucky for me I didn't eat Polly today. Nice of her to warn me, because I don't want to have a pain. Especially not a horrible one, of course."

He got up and wandered along in the direction of his own house.

"Ten times better than Jane!" he ruminated. "I wonder! I bet I'm good to eat then. Jane looks tasty enough, I must be delicious! It's a pity——"

But not even the wolf was stupid enough to consider for very long the possibility of eating himself.

Wolf into Fox

One morning Polly was shopping in Woolworths. She bought a packet of seeds for her garden, a red hair slide, a quarter of a pound of fruit jellies and a pencil. Finally she went to the counter where they sell soap and sponges and shampoos and scent to buy a shampoo for Jane who was having her hair washed that evening.

There was one other customer at the counter, and the sales girl was having a little difficulty with him.

"Well, I don't know about dyeing fur," she was saying doubtfully. "I should think you'd better ask at the household counter."

"Household?" said the customer.

"Down the other end of the store," the sales girl said, and she pointed. "They've got the dyes there for household articles like carpets and fur rugs."

"It's not for carpets or rugs, you stupid girl," the customer said angrily. "It's for me."

"Well, I'm sorry, I'm sure," the girl said, "but I distinctly heard you say fur, so if it isn't a rug or a coat I don't know what you want with fur."

Wolf into Fox

Polly caught the wolf by the elbow just as he opened his mouth to protest and led him towards the household counter.

"It's no good getting angry," she said, soothingly, "she'll never understand that it's real fur and that you really are a wolf; and if she did she'd be so frightened she'd scream and then people would come and catch you and lock you up and all that, and then where should we be? You'd much better let her go on thinking it's a fancy dress and come and buy your dye quietly. What colour do you want, Wolf?"

The wolf allowed himself to be led towards the dyes. They were set out on the household counter in a series of attractive little bottles, each cork tied up with a rag of a different bright colour.

"Aren't they pretty?" said Polly, admiring them. "What sort of colour, Wolf? Look, the bright red is lovely—and so is the jade green. Or, look, Wolf! Do have the purple."

"Don't be so silly," the wolf said sharply. "How could I possibly go about with purple fur?"

"Oh," said Polly. "I'd forgotten it was for you. I'm sorry. No, I suppose you couldn't. Only it is such a gorgeous colour."

"Not purple," said the wolf firmly. "You've never seen a purple fox, have you?"

"No. I've hardly ever seen a fox at all," Polly admitted.

"Well, then."

"But why a fox? I mean, you're a wolf. Why does it matter if foxes aren't purple? You aren't one."

"Not yet," said the wolf. He screwed up his eyes and looked hard at Polly.

"Why are you making a face like that?"

"It's a mysterious face," the wolf said, undoing it again. "It means I'm not going to tell you any more. At present," he added, and made the face again.

Polly knew very well that if you want to get a secret out of someone who doesn't mean to tell it to you, the best way of getting what you want is to pretend to be quite uninterested. Because any one with a secret worth anything is almost as anxious to tell you about it as you are to hear. So she turned away and looked fixedly at the tins of biscuits on the next counter, and hummed a tune to herself.

"I'm not going to tell you any more," the wolf said rather more loudly.

"Good! More about what?"

"About my turning into a fox."

"Oh, are you? I hadn't noticed," Polly said, in what she hoped sounded a very casual way.

Wolf into Fox

"No, you stupid little thing, I haven't started it yet. When I've got the dye, I shall be the right colour for a fox and then you'll see I'll look exactly like one!"

"Why a fox?" Polly couldn't help asking.

"Because they always win. Haven't you noticed in fairy stories and all that sort of thing, the fox is always the clever one? I don't know why," the wolf said, thoughtfully, "but whenever there's any trouble between a wolf and a fox in those old stories, the fox always somehow turns out to be cleverer than the wolf."

"Perhaps foxes are really cleverer than wolves." Polly suggested.

"They're certainly not," the wolf said angrily.

"Then why try to be a fox?"

"I'm not exactly going to be one," the wolf said, "I'm just going to look like one. Then when I'm in a story with you— I mean with anyone I might want to get the better of—I shall look right for being the cleverest of us. And if I look right, I'll feel right. And if I feel right, I shall feel cleverer than you and then I shall eat you up."

"It sounds easy," Polly agreed.

"It is!" the wolf said simply. He turned to the counter and picked out a bottle of reddish brown dye. "I'll have this, please," he said to the sales girl, handing over a sixpenny bit. Then he dropped on to his four feet and ran quickly out of the shop.

For the next day or two Polly looked anxiously about to see the new Fox-Wolf. But as the days passed and there was no sign of him, she began to wonder if perhaps his plans hadn't gone right, if he had had some sort of accident, or was ill. Every large dog of a black or brownish colour that she met, Polly scrutinized carefully: but they all turned out to be nothing but dogs, with no particular interest in Polly.

Ten days or so after her first encounter with the would-be-Fox, Polly was again in Woolworths. This time she was at the ribbon counter, buying two penn'orth of red ribbon, when she heard a well-known voice further down the shop. A shaggy looking person, muffled in a mackintosh was at the household counter, buying five little bottles of reddish brown dye. When he had paid for them and was tucking the bottles into his pockets, Polly stepped up behind him.

"Wolf!" she said.

He gave a great jump, and looked round.

"You shouldn't startle me so," he said reproachfully. "I nearly dropped one of the bottles and there aren't any more. These are the last five they've got. If I broke one of these I might have to wait ages to get any more!"

"But what do you need so many for?" Polly asked. "Wasn't one enough?"

"No," the wolf said. "One wasn't enough. I had to come back the next week and buy two more!"

"Why a week?" Polly asked.

"I was waiting to see what happened."

"What happened to what?"

"What happened to me after I'd taken it."

"But you don't have to wait. You just mix it with water and put the whatever it is you want to dye in, and then you hang it up to dry and then you see. It couldn't take more than about a day."

The wolf looked a little embarrassed.

"I didn't do it quite like that," he said.

"Didn't you mix it with water?"

"Y—yes."

"Perhaps you put in too much. Didn't you read the instructions, Wolf?"

"No, as a matter of fact, I didn't. You see, I sort of forgot to read what it said, and as it was in a bottle it seemed as if it ought to be—as if it was meant—well, in fact, Polly, I did mix it with water and then I drank it all up."

"Oh, Wolf, how awful!" Polly said. "Didn't it make you feel ill?"

"Yes, very ill."

"You might have died, Wolf."

"Yes," said the wolf, looking more cheerful. "You're quite right. But I didn't. And the funny thing is, it didn't turn me reddish brown at all!"

"Not at all?"

"Not so much as a hair of me. So then I read the instructions and I saw I'd made a little mistake."

"A very stupid mistake, Wolf!"

"Not at all. A very understandable mistake. Everyone knows that bottles have drinks in them. Well, anyhow!" he went on in a hurry, "then I read the instructions and I saw I ought to have put myself into it, not it into me. So when I felt better I came to get some more. I got two bottles, but that wasn't nearly enough, so I bought two more. And now if I have all these," he jingled his pockets, "I shall have enough I should think."

"Enough for what?" Polly asked.

"To finish me off."

"Why do you need finishing off?"

They were out of Woolworth's by this time and the wolf

suddenly threw off his mackintosh and said, "Look, Stupid!"

Polly looked. Her once sleek black wolf was now a rather horrid sight. His head and front legs were a fine chestnut brown: they had taken the dye very well indeed: his back legs and tail were the old original black wolf colour, but round his waist he was a disagreeable mixture of both colours.

"You see?" the wolf said. "Even you can't pretend it's exactly a finished job, can you? Now do you understand why I need a few more bottles of dye?"

"You've done your front end, awfully well," Polly said consolingly.

"But what's the good of being a fox one end when I'm still a wolf the other?" the wolf said reasonably. "And it's so embarrassing looking like this. I can't go out without a mackintosh and it's just my luck that all this week the sun has gone on shining and shining so I look almost as silly wearing a mackintosh as I would if I didn't wear it."

"You might look as if you thought it was just going to rain," Polly said comfortingly. "It often does, in England."

"But it hasn't lately. That's just what's so annoying," the wolf said.

"Never mind," Polly said quickly. "Now you can go and finish your back half with the rest of the bottles, and then you'll be able to come out without your mackintosh, and looking like a fox!"

"And then you'd just better watch out, Polly," said the wolf, quite cheered up. "Because I'll be so clever then I'll get you before you can say Wolf Robinson!"

Polly went home and tied up her hair with her red ribbon. She wondered how the wolf was getting on with his dyeing, and she wondered if being fox colour and feeling cleverer would really make any difference to the wolf, or to Polly. She didn't think he'd be much better at catching her, but she thought she had better be careful, and, if possible, clever. She also wondered, as she saw the sun shining brightly every day, whether the poor wolf was still having to wear his mackintosh. He certainly was not in luck: people said the spell of fine weather seemed as if it would go on for ever, and those who had gardens began to complain of drought and to wish for rain.

It was hot and thundery and still dry when Polly, out for a walk by herself, not far from home, suddenly saw a reddish brown shape slink through the bushes at the side of the road, and a moment later a triumphant Fox stood before her: rather larger than life and full of cunning.

"Now, Polly," said the fox-wolf, "this time I really have got you."

Polly looked around. There was no one within call, and the fox-wolf really did look rather convincing. For almost the first time in history, her heart sank.

"You've done it awfully well," she said, as admiringly as she could. "It's beautifully even all over. Sometimes dyeing comes out a bit patchy."

"I haven't any patches at all," the fox-wolf agreed, turning round so that Polly could see the whole of him. "But don't try to take the chance to run away," he added, turning back very quickly.

Polly, to whom the idea had occurred, stood very still. It seemed that this animal was really cleverer than he had been.

"So you've been able to leave off your mackintosh," she said, hoping to delay until she saw some chance of escape.

Wolf into Fox

"Of course. I have nothing to hide," the fox-wolf said in an insufferably self-satisfied tone. He looked down at himself approvingly. "And now, Polly——"

Polly took a step back. The fox-wolf came nearer. Polly opened her mouth to go on with the conversation, which she hoped still to keep on a polite level, when she felt a wet splash on her nose. She looked suspiciously at the fox-wolf and saw a splash arrive on his nose too. Drops as big as half crowns fell rapidly in the dusty path between and all around them. In the distance they heard a faint roll of thunder.

"It's going to rain," Polly said.

"It is raining," the fox-wolf said.

"Hard."

"Very hard."

"You might need your mackintosh."

"I'm not going to bother about that till I've dealt with you," the fox-wolf replied threateningly. He stepped forward again, through what was now a drenching downpour, but hesitated when he saw Polly's face. She was looking first at him and then at the rain and then at the ground round his feet as if she couldn't believe her eyes.

"What is it?" he asked impatiently.

"Oh fox-wolf—Oh Wolf—oh whatever you are, do look!"

"Look at what?"

"The puddle and your fur—oh Wolf you aren't fast dyed! Your colour's all coming off in the rain. You're only half a Fox now, Wolf, and in a minute or two you're going to be just Wolf again and as stupid as ever."

The Animal looked down at the reddish brown puddle round his feet, getting bigger and more reddish brown all the time: and then down at his streaked, spiky brown-black fur, getting blacker as quickly as the water on the ground got red.

"It's coming off!" he muttered stupidly. "But it was supposed to be a Fast Dye!"

"Did you get right into the bath of dye?" Polly asked.

"Right in," said the wolf dejectedly.

"And stayed there for twenty minutes?"

"An hour and a half to make sure!" said the wolf.

"Did you remember to put in a tablespoonful of salt?"

"I used pepper and mustard as well," the wolf said. "The mustard stung my eyes!"

"And did you bring it to the boil!"

"Of course I did."

"And keep it boiling?"

"Of course. I'm not such a fool," the wolf said, "as to

think you can get results if you don't do what the instructions tell you to."

"It must have hurt," Polly said. "You must be awfully brave, Wolf."

"Why?"

"To stay all that time in a bath of boiling dye!"

"Oh, I didn't stay in it when it got too hot," the wolf said cheerfully. "Naturally I got out before I boiled it. You don't expect me to stay in boiling dye, Polly, surely? Not even a Wolf—not even you," he harshly corrected himself, "could be as stupid as that."

"Well," said Polly (she was soaked, but no longer at all frightened). "Now I understand what's happening. Just look at yourself, Wolf."

"Fox," the wolf corrected her.

"Wolf," said Polly firmly. "You're as black as you ever were, the dye's all gone. And I expect all the cleverness has gone too, hasn't it?"

The wolf looked unhappily down at his dripping black fur. If a tear or two fell at the same time it was unnoticeable in so much rain. There was another roll of thunder, closer this time.

"I don't feel my best," he admitted.

"You're very wet and cold, aren't you, Wolf?" Polly urged.

The wolf shivered violently for an answer.

"You feel pretty stupid don't you, Wolf?"

"I don't understand. Fast Dye," the wolf murmured to himself.

"I should get home and have a warm bath and a nice drink of hot cocoa and go straight to bed," Polly said kindly.

"I will," the wolf said, gratefully, turning to trot away.

"And next time you want to be a different colour, try boiling in it," Polly called after him, as she began to run home herself.

"I may be stupid," she heard the wolf say before the next peal of thunder overtook them: and as it died away, "but not as stupid as all that."

The Riddlemaster

———————————

Sitting on one of the public benches in the High Street one warm Saturday morning, Polly licked all round the top of an ice-cream horn.

A large person sat down suddenly beside her. The bench swayed and creaked, and Polly looked round.

"Good morning, Wolf!"

"Good morning, Polly."

"Nice day, Wolf."

"Going to be hot, Polly."

"Mmm," Polly said. She was engaged in trying to save a useful bit of ice-cream with her tongue before it dripped on to the pavement and was wasted.

"In fact it is hot now, Polly."

"I'm not too hot," Polly said.

"Perhaps that delicious looking ice is cooling you down," the wolf said enviously.

"Perhaps it is," Polly agreed.

"I'm absolutely boiling," the wolf said.

Polly fished in the pocket of her cotton dress and pulled out a threepenny bit. It was more than half what she had

left, but she was a kind girl, and in a way she was fond of the wolf, tiresome as he sometimes was.

"Here you are, Wolf," she said, holding it out to him. "Go into Woolworths and get one for yourself."

There was a scurry of feet, a flash of black fur, and a little cloud of white summer dust rose off the pavement near Polly's feet. The wolf had gone.

Two minutes later he came back, a good deal more slowly. He was licking his ice-cream horn with a very long red tongue and it was disappearing extremely quickly. He sat down again beside Polly with a satisfied grunt.

"Mm! Just what I needed. Thank you very much, Polly."

"Not at all, Wolf," said Polly, who had thought that he might have said this before.

The Riddlemaster

She went on licking her ice in a happy dream-like state, while the wolf did the same, but twice as fast.

Presently, in a slightly aggrieved voice, the wolf said, "Haven't you nearly finished?"

"Well no, not nearly," Polly said. She always enjoyed spinning out ices as long as possible. "Have you?"

"Ages ago."

"I wish you wouldn't look at me so hard, Wolf," Polly said, wriggling. "It makes me feel uncomfortable when I'm eating."

"I was only thinking," the wolf said.

"You look sad, then, when you think," Polly remarked.

"I generally am. It's a very sad world, Polly."

"Is it?" said Polly, in surprise.

"Yes. A lot of sad things happen."

"What things?" asked Polly.

"Well, I finish up all my ice-cream."

"That's fairly sad. But at any rate you did have it," Polly said.

"I haven't got it Now," the wolf said. "And it's Now that I want it. Now is the only time to eat ice-cream."

"When you are eating it, it is Now," Polly remarked.

"But when I'm not, it isn't. I wish it was always Now," the wolf sighed.

"It sounds like a riddle," Polly said.

"What does?"

"What you were saying. When is Now not Now or something like that. You know the sort I mean, when is a door not a door?"

"I love riddles," said the wolf in a much more cheerful voice. "I know lots. Let's ask each other riddles."

"Yes, let's," said Polly.

"And I tell you what would make it really amusing. Let's say that whoever wins can eat the other person up."

"Wins how?" Polly asked, cautiously.

"By asking three riddles the other person can't answer."

"Three in a row," Polly insisted.

"Very well. Three in a row."

"And I can stop whenever I want to."

"All right," the wolf agreed, unwillingly. "And I'll start," he added quickly. "What made the penny stamp?"

Polly knew it was because the threepenny bit, and said so. Then she asked the wolf what made the apple turnover, and he knew the answer to that. Polly knew what was the longest word in the dictionary, and the wolf knew what has an eye but cannot see. This reminded him of the question of what has hands, but no fingers and a face but no nose, to which Polly was able to reply that it was a clock.

"My turn," she said, with relief. "Wolf, what gets bigger, the more you take away from it?"

The wolf looked puzzled.

"Are you sure you've got it right, Polly?" he asked at length. "You don't mean it gets smaller the more you take away from it?"

"No, I don't."

"It gets bigger?"

"Yes."

"No cake I ever saw did that," the wolf said, thinking aloud. "Some special kind of pudding, perhaps?"

"It's not a pudding," Polly said.

"I know!" the wolf said triumphantly. "It's the sort of pain you get when you're hungry. And the more you don't eat the worse the pain gets. That's getting bigger the less you do about it."

"No, you're wrong," Polly said. "It isn't a pain or anything to eat, either. It's a hole. The more you take away, the bigger it gets, don't you see, Wolf?"

"Being hungry is a sort of hole in your inside," the wolf said. "But anyhow it's my turn now. I'm going to ask you a new riddle, so you won't know the answer already, and I don't suppose you'll be able to guess it, either. What gets filled up three or four times a day, and yet can always hold more?"

"Do you mean it can hold more after it's been filled?" Polly asked.

The wolf thought, and then said, "Yes".

"But it couldn't, Wolf! If it was really properly filled up it couldn't hold any more."

"It does though," the wolf said triumphantly. "It seems to be quite bursting full and then you try very hard and it still holds a little more."

Polly had her suspicions of what this might be, but she didn't want to say in case she was wrong.

"I can't guess."

"It's me!" the wolf cried, in delight. "Got you, that time, Polly! However full up I am, I can always manage a little bit more. Your turn next, Polly."

"What," Polly asked, "is the difference between an elephant and a pillar-box?"

The wolf thought for some time.

"The elephant is bigger," he said, at last.

"Yes. But that isn't the right answer."

"The pillar-box is red. Bright red. And the elephant isn't."

"Ye-es. But that isn't the right answer either."

The wolf looked puzzled. He stared hard at the old-fashioned Victorian pillar-box in the High Street. It had a crimped lid with a knob on top like a silver teapot. But it didn't help him. After some time he said crossly, "I don't know."

"You mean you can't tell the difference between an elephant and a pillar-box?"

"No."

"Then I shan't send you to post my letters," Polly said, triumphantly. She thought this was a very funny riddle.

The wolf, however, didn't.

"You don't see the joke, Wolf?" Polly asked, a little disappointed that he was so unmoved.

"I see it, yes. But I don't think it's funny. It's not a proper riddle at all. It's just silly."

"Now you ask me something," Polly suggested. After a minute or two's thought, the wolf said, "What is the difference between pea soup and a clean pocket handkerchief?"

"Pea soup is hot and a pocket handkerchief is cold," said Polly.

"No. Anyhow you could have cold pea soup."

"Pea soup is green," said Polly.

"I expect a clean pocket handkerchief could be green too, if it tried," said the wolf. "Do you give it up?"

"Well," said Polly, "of course I do know the difference, but I don't know what you want me to say."

"I want you to say you don't know the difference between them," said the wolf, crossly.

"But I do," said Polly.

"But then I can't say what I was going to say!" the wolf cried.

He looked so much disappointed that Polly relented.

"All right, then, you say it."

"You don't know the difference between pea soup and a clean pocket handkerchief?"

"I'll pretend I don't. No, then," said Polly.

"You ought to be more careful what you keep in your pockets," the wolf said. He laughed so much at this that he choked, and Polly had to beat him hard on the back before he recovered and could sit back comfortably on the seat again.

"Your turn," he said, as soon as he could speak.

Polly thought carefully. She thought of a riddle about a man going to St. Ives; of one about the man who showed a portrait to another man; of one about a candle; but she was not satisfied with any of them. With so many riddles it isn't really so much a question of guessing the answers, as of knowing them or not knowing them already, and if the wolf were to invent a completely new riddle out of his head, he would be able to eat her, Polly, in no time at all.

"Hurry up," said the wolf.

Perhaps it was seeing his long red tongue at such very close quarters, or it may have been the feeling that she had no time to lose, that made Polly say, before she had considered what she was going to say, "What is it that has teeth, but no mouth?"

"Grrrr," said the wolf, showing all his teeth for a moment. "Are you quite sure he hasn't a mouth, Polly?"

"Quite sure. And I'm supposed to be asking the questions, not you, Wolf."

The wolf did not appear to hear this. He had now turned his back on Polly and was going through some sort of rapid repetition in a subdued gabble, through which Polly could hear only occasional words.

". . . Grandma, so I said the better to see you with, gabble, gabble, gabble, Ears you've got, gabble gabble better to hear gabble gabble gabble gabble gabble TEETH gabble eat you all up."

He turned round with a satisfied air.

"I've guessed it Polly. It's a GRANDMOTHER."

"No," said Polly astonished.

"Well then, Red Riding Hood's grandmother if you are so particular. The story mentions her eyes and her ears and her teeth, so I expect she hadn't got anything else. No mouth anyhow."

"It's not anyone's grandmother."

"Not a grandmother," said the wolf slowly. He shook his head. "It's difficult. Tell me some more about it. Are they sharp teeth, Polly?"

"They can be," Polly said.

"As sharp as mine?" asked the wolf, showing his for comparison.

"No," said Polly, drawing back a little. "But more tidily arranged," she added.

The wolf shut his jaws with a snap.

"I give up," he said, in a disagreeable tone. "There isn't anything I know of that has teeth and no mouth. What use would the teeth be to anyone without a mouth? I mean, what is the point of taking a nice juicy bite out of something if you've got to find someone else's mouth to swallow it for you? It doesn't make sense."

"It's a comb," said Polly, when she got a chance to speak.

"A what?" cried the wolf in disgust.

"A COMB. What you do your hair with. It's got teeth, hasn't it? But no mouth. A comb, Wolf."

The wolf looked sulky. Then he said in a bright voice, "My turn now, and I'll begin straight away. What is the difference between a nice fat young pink pig and a plate of sausages and bacon? You don't know, of course, so I'll tell you. It's——"

"Wolf!" Polly interrupted.

"It's a very good riddle, this one, and I can't blame you for not having guessed it. The answer is——"

"WOLF!" Polly said, "I want to tell you something."

"Not the answer?"

"No. Not the answer. Something else."

"Well, go on."

"Look, Wolf, we made a bargain, didn't we, that whoever lost three lives running by not being able to answer riddles, might be eaten up by the other person?"

"Yes," the wolf agreed. "And you've lost two already, and now you're not going to be able to answer the third and then I shall eat you up. Now I'll tell you what the difference is between a nice fat little pink——"

"NO!" Polly shouted. "Listen, Wolf! I may have lost two lives already, but you have lost three!"

"I haven't!"

"Yes, you have! You couldn't answer the riddle about the hole, you didn't know the difference between an elephant and a pillar-box——"

"I do!" said the wolf indignantly.

"Well, you may now, but you didn't when I asked you the riddle; and you didn't know about the comb having teeth and no mouth. That was three you couldn't answer in a row, so it isn't you that is going to eat me up."

"What is it then?" the wolf asked, shaken.

"It's me that is going to eat you up!" said Polly.

The wolf moved rather further away.

"Are you really going to eat me up, Polly?"

"In a moment, Wolf. I'm just considering how I'll have you cooked," said Polly.

"I'm very tough, Polly."

"That's all right, Wolf. I can simmer you gently over a low flame until you are tender."

"I don't suppose I'd fit very nicely into any of your saucepans, Polly."

"I can use the big one Mother has for making jam. That's an enormous saucepan," said Polly, thoughtfully, measuring the wolf with her eyes.

The wolf began visibly to shake where he sat.

"Oh please, Polly, don't eat me. Don't eat me up this time," he urged. "Let me off this once, I promise I'll never do it again."

"Never do what again?" Polly asked.

"I don't know. What was I doing?" the wolf asked himself, in despair.

"Trying to get me to eat," Polly suggested.

"Well, of course, I'm always doing that," the wolf agreed.

"And you would have eaten me?" Polly asked.

"Not if you'd asked very nicely, I wouldn't," the wolf said. "Like I'm asking now."

"And if I didn't eat you up, you'd stop trying to get me?"

The wolf considered.

"Look," he said, "I can't say I'll stop for ever, because after all a wolf is a wolf, and if I promised to stop for ever I wouldn't be a wolf any more. But I promise to stop for a

long time. I won't try any more today."

"And what about after today?" Polly insisted.

"The first time I catch you," the wolf said dreamily, "if you ask *very* nicely I'll let you go because you've let me off today. But after that, no mercy! It'll be just Snap! Crunch! Swallow!"

"All right," Polly said, recollecting that so far the wolf had not ever got as far as catching her successfully even once. "You can go."

The wolf ducked his head gratefully and trotted off. Polly saw him threading his way between the busy shoppers in the High Street.

But she sat contentedly in the hot sun and wondered what was the difference between a fat pink pig and a plate of sausages and bacon. Not much, if she knew her wolf!

The Kidnapping

One day Polly was in the kitchen, washing up dreamily at the sink. Outside the sun was shining hot and bright, and a delicious smell of newly-cut grass came in through the open window. Bert, the odd job man, was piling up the grass cuttings in a corner of the garden to make a compost heap; Lucy, Polly's little sister, was helping him, or thought she was helping, by carrying small piles of grass to and fro, sometimes in the right direction, but more often in the wrong one.

"Bert," said a voice from the other side of the house. "Bert! Come here a minute, will you?"

"Wharris'it?" Bert called back: but he went on piling up his compost heap.

"See you about something very important!" the voice said urgently.

Polly could see Bert say Bother: she couldn't hear it, but the way he put down the rake showed exactly how he was feeling. Then he went off along the path in the direction of the voice. Lucy, alone in the back garden, filled a small tin pail with gravel and wandered over the lawn, sprinkling it with little stones.

Suddenly a large black Something jumped over the garden wall, snatched up Lucy and was off again before Polly had quite realized what was happening. But she knew directly who it had been. Only the wolf would come into the garden like that and steal small fat Lucy. For what? It was a horrible thought.

For the first time in all her dealings with the wolf, Polly was frightened. But she knew she must do something quickly, so she ran out of the kitchen, without even waiting to dry her hands, out through the garden and into the hot dusty road outside.

The Kidnapping

She looked up and down, but there was no one in sight. A scatter of small pebbles led off to the right.

"He must have gone home," Polly thought. "He wouldn't take Lucy anywhere she'd be recognized, it wouldn't be safe for him."

The pebbles led in the direction of the wolf's house. Polly had never gone that way alone before, and she didn't much like doing it now, but the thought of Lucy in the wolf's power drove her on.

Outside the wolf's door she stopped. She wasn't sure how she was going to get Lucy out; she had no plans and she didn't want to have to go into the house herself. She put up her hand to ring the door-bell; then she took it down again. She actually lifted the knocker, but let it fall back silently. Polly, for once, was at a loss.

She was just summoning her courage to let the wolf know she had arrived, when something went hurtling past her head. Someone inside the house had thrown a stick out of the window just beside the porch, and it had only just missed hitting her in the face. A moment later a large black body followed the stick out of the window. The wolf retrieved the stick and jumped neatly back through the window again.

"Good Dog," Polly heard Lucy's voice saying, "fetch stick."

"I'm not a dog, you Silly little girl," the wolf's voice said crossly. "I'm a Wolf, and I'm going to——"

"More," said Lucy. She always said more for something she had enjoyed the first time—more cake, more dance, more Red Riding Hood. The stick flew out of the window again, this time further from Polly's head.

The Kidnapping

"Fetch stick! Good dog!"

The wolf came, rather more slowly, out of the window and went back again with the stick in his mouth.

"Clever dog," Lucy said approvingly.

"You're stupid," the wolf said, really annoyed. "You're almost as stupid as Polly. Listen, stupid little Lucy, I'm NOT a dog, I'm a Wolf, and I'm going to eat you all up."

"Good wolf," said Lucy contentedly. "Fetch stick."

For the third time the stick came out and was fetched by a reluctant and now definitely sulky wolf. As he landed inside the room again, he turned and slammed the bottom of the window down hard.

"Now you can't throw the stick out again," he said. "You can't reach up to the top opening. Now do listen properly, Lucy. I am not a dog, do you understand?"

"Not dog," said Lucy agreeably.

Polly moved up to the window and peered in. It was not a very comfortable looking room, a sort of parlour, furnished stiffly and scantily, with hard knobbly-looking chairs and a shiny horsehair sofa. A large dog basket containing a piece of striped blanket near the fireplace seemed to indicate that the wolf sometimes slept here; there was a round table in the middle of the room, partly covered by a red woollen crochet mat.

Lucy was sitting comfortably in the dog-basket. She had discovered a hole in the stripy blanket and she was picking at the edges and enlarging it with apparent satisfaction. The wolf was sitting at the table, looking annoyed, tapping on the table, biting his nails, and showing every sign of being anxious and jumpy.

"I am NOT a dog, Lucy," he said again, impressively.

The Kidnapping

Lucy took no notice of this remark.

"I am a Wolf."

"Wolf," Lucy agreed. She stuck her thumb through the hole in the blanket and said, "Look! Thumb!"

"I am a Wolf and I'm going to eat you all up."

This was a game with which Lucy was quite familiar. She climbed out of the basket and approached the wolf with her mouth wide open.

"Eat you all up," she repeated, and, reaching the wolf, sank her small sharp teeth into his front left leg.

"Ow! Wow!" the wolf said indignantly, pulling away from her sharply, "don't do that! It hurts, you horrible little creature!" He nursed his wounded limb tenderly with the other paw and looked at Lucy in hurt surprise.

The Kidnapping

But Lucy was delighted. She had seldom had a playfellow who acted pain and surprise so well, and she was encouraged to improve on her efforts. She walked round behind the wolf, saw his irresistible feathery tail hanging out between the bars of the chair, and gave it a sharp pull.

The wolf turned round with a yelp of astonishment and pain.

"Eat you all up," said Lucy, opening her mouth at him again and laughing heartily. She made another successful snap at his other front paw.

"You beastly little girl," the wolf said, now nearly in tears. "You don't understand the simplest remark. I didn't bring you here to bite me and pull my tail and make me do stupid, useless things like jumping in and out of windows to fetch your horrid stick as if I was a tame dog. Can't you see it isn't you that's going to eat me up, it's me that is going to eat you up. Now. For my lunch. No," he added, looking at the marble pillared clock on the mantelpiece, which permanently told the time of a quarter past four. "For my tea."

"Tea," said Lucy. She was rather like an echo sometimes, picking on the one familiar word out of a long speech. "Lucy's tea."

"Not for you," the wolf said firmly.

"TEA," said Lucy, equally firmly and a good deal louder.

"No tea for you. For me," the wolf explained.

"TEA," said Lucy at the top of her voice. Her face suddenly grew brick red and her mouth went square. An enormous tear rolled down her cheek and made a considerable pool on the oilcloth floor.

"Don't cry!" the wolf said, alarmed, "for goodness' sake don't cry. And don't shriek. Someone might hear, and anyhow I can't bear children who cry, it makes me go funny all over."

"Tea," Lucy said, in a quieter voice, but the wolf recognized the dangers of delay.

"Yes, yes," he said soothingly, "tea for Lucy."

"Lucy's chair," said Lucy, climbing up and sitting on it expectantly. No more tears appeared, and her colour was miraculously restored to normal.

"That's the chair I always sit on," the wolf complained.

"LUCY'S CHAIR," Lucy said: her colour began to rise, alarmingly and her mouth began to set into corners.

"Yes, yes, Lucy's chair." The wolf pulled a sort of cross-legged stool up to the table and sat on it, trying to look as if he were enjoying himself.

"Butter," Lucy demanded.

The wolf slipped off his stool and disappeared out of the door. When he came back a minute or two later, he was carrying a tray on which he seemed to have loaded everything he could think of that Lucy could possibly want for tea. There was a large brown steaming teapot, a rusty battered kettle, a sugar bowl, a chipped mug with a picture of an engine on it, a cocoa tin with no lid, half full of biscuits, a plastic plate, the end of a brown loaf, and a sizeable piece of butter in a green soap dish. He put the tray on the table and looked at Lucy nervously.

"Tea," said Lucy approvingly. She leant forward and seized the mug, looked into it, found it empty, and held it out to the wolf.

"Tea," she said again. "Lucy's tea. Butter."

The wolf hastily picked up the teapot in a paw that trembled slightly and tipped it to pour into the mug. But when Lucy saw the colour of the liquid that came out of the spout, her face changed.

"Tea!" she said in disgust. "No tea. Milk!"

She took the mug away just before the wolf removed the teapot. A stream of nearly boiling tea cascaded down to the floor and splashed on his foot.

"Ow! That hurts! You've made me hurt my foot," he cried reproachfully. But Lucy was not interested in the wolf's troubles.

"MILK," was all she said, but the wolf knew better now than to delay. He left the room and was back again with a jug of milk quicker than Polly would have believed possible. He filled Lucy's mug, and she drank thirstily, and then held out the mug again for more.

"But this is all I've got," the wolf pleaded. "The milkman doesn't call again until tomorrow, and I meant to make a milk pudding for supper."

"MORE MILK," Lucy said.

"I'll just keep enough to put in my tea," the wolf said, apologetically, pouring out about half the mugful.

"MORE," said Lucy. "Lucy thirsty," she explained in a friendly way, as she drained the last remnants of the unfortunate wolf's milk supply. She looked round the table for further replenishment. "Butter."

The wolf, obviously at the end of his resources, pushed the soap dish towards her. Lucy frowned.

"Bread 'n Butter," she said, clearly pitying anyone who did not understand the simplest rules of behaviour.

The wolf cut a large slice of bread and spread it with a moderate supply of butter. Lucy took it, and began to lick the butter. The wolf stared at her in horror. He sat in a stupefied silence till Lucy, having licked the bread quite dry of its butter, held it out to him and said emphatically, "More".

"More?" said the wolf. He could hardly believe his ears.

"More Butter," said Lucy impatiently.

"But you haven't eaten the bread. I mean to say, people don't just go on having more butter on the same piece of bread. That isn't what bread and butter means," the wolf protested.

"MORE BUTTER."

"Oh, very well. Have it your own way." The wolf spread a generous layer of butter on the slice of bread and handed it back to Lucy.

He poured himself out a cup of bitter black tea. There was no milk left, so he sweetened it liberally with sugar, and began to drink, making a face as he tasted how nasty it was. But Lucy had noticed his last action and had had a new idea.

"Sugar," she said, dropping her bread, now licked nearly clean again, on the floor. She held out her hand for the sugar basin.

"No," said the wolf, with unusual firmness. "I'm not going to let you polish off all my sugar." He hid the sugar basin behind him, on his stool. "Have a biscuit?" He held the cocoa tin out towards Lucy.

Lucy looked doubtfully into the tin.

"Choc bikkit?" she inquired.

"No—o—but there's a very nice one here. Look!" and the wolf held up a crumbling Oval Osborne.

"No bikkit," said Lucy.

"Nice biscuit," said the wolf.

"No bikkit."

"No, no. Certainly. It's a repellent biscuit," the wolf said, putting it back in the cocoa tin. "You don't want a nasty biscuit like that. I'll find you a really good biscuit this time."

He scrabbled busily about at the bottom of the tin, then produced the same biscuit and held it out to Lucy invitingly.

"Sugar," said Lucy.

"No," said the wolf.

"SUGAR."

"No."

Lucy abandoned this unprofitable conversation and looked round the room for inspiration.

"Lucy have a apple?" she asked politely.

"I haven't got any apples," the wolf replied.

"Banana?"

"I haven't any bananas."

"Then I have Bun," Lucy said decisively. She was sure there could be no one who couldn't produce at least Bun, even if they were so unfortunate as not to have apples and bananas.

"I haven't got—" the wolf began, but he changed his mind. He was reluctantly learning a little cunning too. He looked into the biscuit tin for the third time and gave a start of well-acted surprise.

"Why, what's this?" he cried, "I was just going to say I hadn't got any buns, but there's one left at the bottom of the tin."

He held the Oval Osborne biscuit out to Lucy in a trembling paw. She gave him an enchanting smile and took it.

"Gank you."

It seemed to Polly that this was the moment to ring the front door bell. She pressed it firmly, and kept her finger there for some time.

The Kidnapping

The door was opened abruptly. An exhausted, frayed wolf, visibly at his last resources, stood before her.

"Polly!" he said, "you've come in the nick of time. Another five minutes and I don't know what I should have done. For goodness' sake come in and take her away before she eats up everything I've got in the house. Do you know," he went on, trembling with rage, as he led the way from the front door to the room where Lucy was finishing her biscuit, "that she even tried to eat me?"

Lucy was sitting comfortably and crumbily on the wolf's special chair when Polly came into the room. She looked at Polly without any special surprise and said agreeably, "Good morning, Polly". She always said, "Good morning," whatever the time of the day, finding it easier to pronounce than, "Good afternoon".

"I've come to take you home," Polly said. She had decided to pretend that the whole affair had been carried on under the politest circumstances. "Get down from your chair, Lucy, and thank the kind wolf for asking you to tea."

Lucy obediently struggled off the chair and made for the door as fast as she could.

"Say thank you," Polly reminded her as they reached the front door again.

"Gank you, Wolf," Lucy said, "Lucy come back soon."

"Not too soon," the wolf pleaded. He looked very limp as he held the door open for them to go out.

"And now," Lucy said, as, holding Polly's hand she trotted down the short garden path. "Lucy go home and have TEA."

Behind her Polly heard the wolf groan. He had at last met his match.

Other titles in Jane Nissen Books

A TRAVELLER IN TIME
By Alison Uttley
Illustrated by Faith Jaques
Foreword by Margaret Mahy
ISBN 978 1 903252 27 7

ASK ME NO QUESTIONS
By Ann Schlee
Foreword by Jamila Gavin
ISBN 978 1 903252 26 0

A STRONG AND WILLING GIRL
By Dorothy Edwards
Illustrated by Robert Micklewright
Foreword by Jacqueline Wilson
ISBN 978 1 903252 20 8

BOGWOPPIT
By Ursula Moray Williams
Illustrated by Shirley Hughes
Foreword by Shirley Hughes
ISBN 978 1 903252 36 9

BRENDON CHASE
By B.B.
Illustrated by Denys Watkins-Pitchford
Foreword by Philip Pullman
ISBN 978 1 903252 00 0

BUNCHY
By Joyce Lankester Brisley
Illustrated by the author
Foreword by Fiona Waters
ISBN 978 1 903252 22 2

CHRISTMAS WITH THE SAVAGES
By Mary Clive
Illustrated by Philip Gough
Foreword by Laura Cecil
ISBN 978 1 903252 31 4

CIRCUS SHOES
By Noel Streatfeild
Illustrated by Clarke Hutton
Foreword by Gillian Cross
ISBN 978 1 903252 25 3

FATTYPUFFS AND THINIFERS
By André Maurois
Illustrated by Fritz Wegner
Foreword by Raymond Briggs
ISBN 978 1 903252 07 9

GREEN SMOKE
By Rosemary Manning
Illustrated by Constance Marshall
Foreword by Amanda Craig
ISBN 978 1 903252 29 1

JOHNNY'S BAD DAY
By Edward Ardizzone
Illustrated by the author
ISBN 978 1 903252 30 7

KINGS AND QUEENS
Poems by Eleanor and Herbert Farjeon
Illustrated by Robin Jacques
With a letter from the Queen Mother
ISBN 978 1 903252 12 3

MAGIC IN MY POCKET
By Alison Uttley
Illustrated by Judith Brook
Foreword by Margaret Clark
ISBN 978 1 903252 17 8

MRS COCKLE'S CAT
By Philippa Pearce
Illustrated by Antony Maitland
Foreword by Frank Cottrell Boyce
ISBN 978 1 903252 33 8

MY FRIEND MR LEAKEY
By J.B.S Haldane
Illustrated and with a Foreword by
Quentin Blake
ISBN 978 1 903252 19 2

OLD PETER'S RUSSIAN TALES
By Arthur Ransome
Illustrated by Faith Jaques
Foreword by Christina Hardyment
ISBN 978 1 903252 16 1

STARS OF FORTUNE
By Cynthia Harnett
Illustrated by the author
Foreword by Amanda Craig
ISBN 978 1 903252 24 6

TENNIS SHOES
By Noel Streatfeild
Illustrated by D.L. Mays
Foreword by Adèle Geras
ISBN 978 1 903252 08 6

THEATRE SHOES
By Noel Streatfeild
Illustrated by D.L Mays
Foreword by Eleanor Updale
ISBN 978 1 903252 32 1

THE COUNTRY CHILD
By Alison Uttley
Illustrated by C.F.Tunnicliffe, R.A.
Foreword by Nina Bawden
ISBN 978 1 903252 01 7

THE CUCKOO CLOCK
By Mrs Molesworth
Illustrated by E.H. Shepard
Foreword by Emma Chichester Clark
ISBN 978 1 903252 14 7

THE HOUSE IN NORHAM GARDENS
By Penelope Lively
Foreword by Philip Pullman
ISBN 978 1 903252 18 5

THE LARK AND THE LAUREL
By Barbara Willard
Illustrated by Gareth Floyd
Foreword by Kenneth Crossley-Holland
ISBN 978 1 903252 34 5

THE MAGIC CITY
By E. Nesbit
Illustrated by H. R. Millar
Foreword by Mary Hoffman
ISBN 978 1 903252 37 6

THE SPRIG OF BROOM
By Barbara Willard
Illustrated by Gareth Floyd
Foreword by Kevin Crossley-Holland
ISBN 978 1 903252 35 2

THE ORDINARY PRINCESS
By M.M. Kaye
Illustrated by the author
Foreword by Bel Mooney
ISBN 978 1 903252 13 0

THE TAIL OF THE TRINOSAUR
By Charles Causley
Illustrated by Jill Gardiner
Foreword by Michael Rosen
ISBN 978 1 903252 23 9

THE VOYAGE OF QV 66
By Penelope Lively
Illustrated by Harold Jones
Foreword by Michael Morpurgo
ISBN 978 1 903252 21 5

THE WIND ON THE MOON
By Eric Linklater
Illustrated by Nicolas Bentley
Foreword by Lindsey Fraser
ISBN 978 1 903252 02 4

THE WOODS OF WINDRI
By Violet Needham
Illustrated by Joyce Bruce
Foreword by Stephanie Nettell
ISBN 978 1 903252 15 4